# RAMA EARNS A TITLE

LONG AGO, A WISE YOUTH CALLED RAMA WAS PLAYING WITH HIS FRIENDS.

SUDDENLY AN OLD WOMAN CAME BY.

SUCH MISFORTUNE COULD ONLY BEFALL A WIDOW. IF ONLY I HAD SOMEONE TO FIGHT FOR ME, WOULD THE JUDGE DARE PASS SUCH AN UNJUST VERDICT?

RAMA WAS MOVED.

WHAT'S THE MATTER, MOTHER? WHY ARE YOU WAILING?

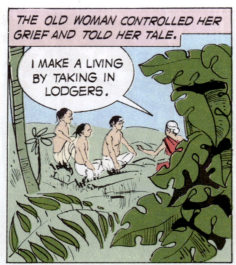

THE OLD WOMAN CONTROLLED HER GRIEF AND TOLD HER TALE.

I MAKE A LIVING BY TAKING IN LODGERS.

"ONE DAY, FOUR OF MY LODGERS CAME TO ME WITH A SEALED POT.

MOTHER, PLEASE KEEP THIS FOR US.

"I TOOK THE POT. AND REMEMBER, MOTHER, IT SHOULD BE RETURNED ONLY IF ALL FOUR OF US TOGETHER ASK FOR IT.

"A FEW DAYS LATER, AS THE FOUR OF THEM WERE SITTING OUTSIDE THE HOUSE—

BUTTERMILK! DELICIOUS BUTTERMILK!

"THE YOUNGEST OF THEM CAME IN.

MY FRIENDS HAVE SENT ME IN TO ASK FOR THE BRASS POT WE LEFT WITH YOU.

I'M SORRY. I CAN'T GIVE IT UNLESS ALL FOUR OF YOU ASK FOR IT.

WELL, MY FRIENDS ARE OUTSIDE. YOU CAN CHECK WITH THEM.

HEY, YOU OUT THERE! YOUR FRIEND SAYS YOU'VE SENT HIM IN FOR THE POT. SHALL I GIVE IT TO HIM?

YES! YES! AND BE QUICK ABOUT IT.

HOW WAS I TO KNOW THAT THEY HAD SENT THEIR YOUNG FRIEND IN TO FETCH AN EMPTY POT TO BUY BUTTERMILK IN?

I UNDERSTAND. PLEASE CONTINUE, MOTHER. WHAT HAPPENED AFTER THAT?

"I GAVE THE POT TO THE ROGUE.

HERE, TAKE IT. YOUR FRIENDS ARE IMPATIENT FOR IT.

"HE TOOK THE POT AND WENT OUT THROUGH THE BACK DOOR. I WAS PUZZELED.

WHY IS HE USING THE BACK DOOR? WELL, IT'S NO CONCERN OF MINE!

"A LITTLE LATER, THE THREE OUT-SIDE CAME IN.

WHAT IS THAT FOOL DOING? WHERE IS THE POT?

OH, I'VE GIVEN IT TO YOUR FRIEND, SEAL INTACT. HE TOOK IT OUT THROUGH THE BACK DOOR.

SEAL INTACT! WHICH POT DID YOU GIVE HIM?

WHY! THE POT YOU HAD ASKED ME TO KEEP. HASN'T HE BROUGHT IT TO YOU?

"TO MY SURPRISE, THEY WERE FURIOUS.

FOOLISH WOMAN! YOU'LL PAY FOR THIS, YOU OLD HAG!

"THEY DRAGGED ME OUT...

"... TO THE CITY JUDGE AND TOLD HIM THEIR STORY.

SHE HAD STRICT INSTRUCTIONS NOT TO PART WITH THE POT UNTIL ALL FOUR OF US JOINTLY ASKED FOR IT.

BUT THEY DID. I MEAN THEY SENT THE ROGUE IN. I EVEN CHECKED WITH THEM. THEY...

"THE JUDGE REFUSED TO HEAR ME OUT."

SILENCE, WOMAN. THE FOUR LODGERS DID NOT JOINTLY ASK YOU FOR IT. YOU ARE GUILTY. EITHER RETURN THE POT OR BE PREPARED TO GO TO PRISON.

5

RAMA WAS LOST IN THOUGHT.

THE LODGERS MUST HAVE BEEN THIEVES AND THE POT CONTAINED THEIR LOOT. NOW THEY WANT TO MAKE THIS POOR WIDOW PAY FOR THEIR FOLLY.

HE WAS DISGUSTED WITH THE JUDGE AND EVEN MORE WITH HIS KING.

FIE ON OUR KING WHO RELIES ON SUCH AN UNFAIR JUDGE.

THE KING'S MEN WHO WERE PASSING BY HEARD HIS REMARK.

HOW DARE THAT BRAT RAISE HIS VOICE AGAINST THE KING!

THEY CAUGHT RAMA...

... AND DRAGGED HIM BEFORE THE KING.

WHEN THE KING LEARNT WHY RAMA HAD BEEN BROUGHT BEFORE HIM, HE WAS AMUSED.

WELL, MY SON! TAKE THE JUDGE'S SEAT AND SEE IF YOU CAN DO BETTER.

RAMA STEPPED BOLDLY UP AND TOOK THE SEAT.

SUMMON THE PARTIES.

WHEN THE PARTIES WERE SUMMONED AND THEIR STATEMENTS RECORDED, RAMA PRONOUNCED HIS VERDICT.

THE PLAINTIFFS HAVE NO CASE. UNLESS ALL FOUR OF THEM ASK FOR THE POT, HOW CAN THE WIDOW PART WITH IT?

LET THEM PRODUCE THE FOURTH FELLOW AND THE WIDOW WILL GIVE THEM THE POT.

THE KING WAS ASTOUNDED BY THIS REMARKABLE DISPLAY OF WISDOM.

MY SON, I CONFER ON YOU THE TITLE OF CITY JUDGE.

FROM THAT DAY RAMA CAME TO BE KNOWN AS MARYADA RAMA OR RAMA THE JUST.

# THE FALSE WITNESSES TRAPPED

ONCE, TWO MEN CAME TO MARYADA RAMA.

RAMA FIRST HEARD THE PLAINTIFF.

SIR, I HAD A VALUABLE RUBY WHICH I LEFT WITH THIS MAN FOR SAFE-KEEPING WHEN I WENT ON A PILGRIMAGE FOUR YEARS AGO.

NOW HE REFUSES TO GIVE IT BACK.

9

BUT I'VE RETURNED IT TO HIM, SIR, IN THE PRESENCE OF THREE WITNESSES.

THAT'S A LIE, SIR.

SUMMON THE WITNESSES.

THE DEFENDANT HAD BRIBED HIS OWN WASHERMAN, BARBER AND COOK TO COME AND SUPPORT HIS STORY.

DID YOU SEE THE PRECIOUS STONE BEING RETURNED?

YES, SIR.

RAMA TURNED TO HIS ATTENDANT.

GIVE ALL FIVE OF THEM SOME CLAY AND ASK EACH OF THEM TO MAKE A MODEL OF THE PRECIOUS STONE.

WHEN THE MODELS ARE READY SEND THEM TO ME.

THE PLAINTIFF AND THE DEFENDANT HAD NO PROBLEM. THEY KNEW THAT THE PRECIOUS STONE WAS A RUBY AND GOT DOWN TO WORK ON THEIR MODELS.

BUT THE FALSE WITNESSES WHO HAD NEVER SEEN THE RUBY, DID NOT KNOW WHAT TO DO. SO EACH OF THEM MADE A MODEL OF WHAT WAS TO HIM A PRECIOUS STONE—THE STONE USED IN HIS TRADE.

THE STONE ON WHICH I WASH MY CLOTHES IS THE MOST PRECIOUS STONE.

THAT'S IT! IT MUST HAVE BEEN A WHET-STONE. WHAT STONE COULD BE MORE PRE-CIOUS!

THE PRECIOUS STONE IN QUESTION CANNOT BE ANYTHING ELSE BUT A QUERN*

* STONE FOR GRINDING SPICES.

WHEN THE FIVE MODELS WERE PLACED BEFORE RAMA—

THESE MODELS PROVE THAT THE WITNESSES ARE LYING. THEY HAVE NEVER SEEN THE RUBY.

HE LOOKED STERNLY AT THE DEFENDANT.

THESE WITNESSES HAVE BEEN HIRED BY YOU.

YOU AND YOUR WITNESSES SHALL BE PUNISHED FOR PERJURY, AFTER THE RUBY IS RETURNED TO THE PLAINTIFF, ITS RIGHTFUL OWNER.

# THE FOWL THIEF

A WOMAN'S HEN ONCE STRAYED INTO HER GREEDY NEIGHBOUR'S HOUSE.

AH! I SHALL HAVE ROAST CHICKEN FOR LUNCH.

AT DUSK, THE OWNER OF THE FOWL BECAME ANXIOUS.

MY HEN HAS NOT RETURNED YET. I'D BETTER GO AND FETCH HER.

SHE WENT TO HER NEIGHBOUR'S HOUSE.

WHERE IS MY HEN? I SAW HER STRAYING IN HERE A FEW HOURS BACK.

I DON'T KNOW WHAT YOU ARE TALKING ABOUT.

WHAT ELSE BUT MY HEN? RETURN IT OR I'LL GO AND LODGE A COMPLAINT AGAINST YOU.

I'VE NEVER SET EYES ON YOUR HEN. I'M NOT AFRAID OF YOUR THREATS.

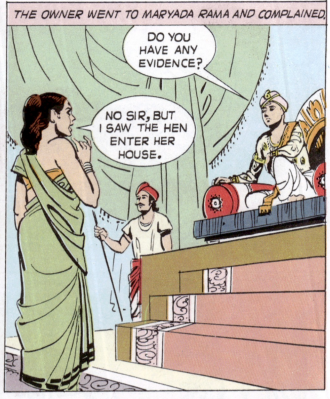

THE OWNER WENT TO MARYADA RAMA AND COMPLAINED.

DO YOU HAVE ANY EVIDENCE?

NO SIR, BUT I SAW THE HEN ENTER HER HOUSE.

RAMA SENT FOR THE NEIGHBOUR.

YOU ARE UNDER OATH. NOW TELL ME THE TRUTH.

BELIEVE ME, SIR. I DON'T KNOW WHAT SHE'S TALKING ABOUT. YOU CAN SEARCH MY HOUSE.

RAMA WAS INCLINED TO BELIEVE THE PLAINTIFF'S STORY BUT THERE WAS NO PROOF OF THE SUSPECT'S GUILT.

I'M SURE SHE'S COOKED THE FOWL AND EATEN IT. I'LL GET THE TRUTH OUT OF HER YET.

HE PRETENDED TO WEIGH THE MATTER CAREFULLY. THEN—

YOU MAY GO NOW. I'LL GIVE YOU THE VERDICT TOMORROW.

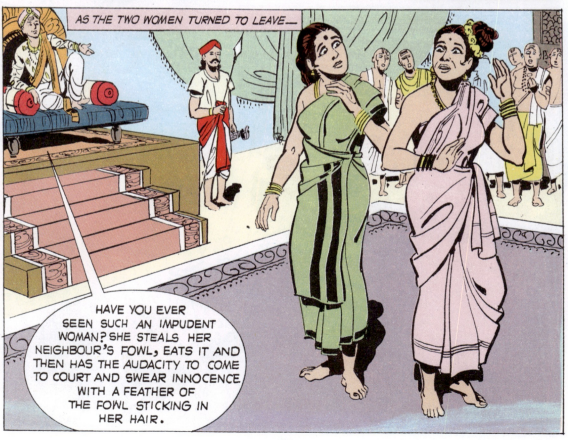

AS THE TWO WOMEN TURNED TO LEAVE—

HAVE YOU EVER SEEN SUCH AN IMPUDENT WOMAN? SHE STEALS HER NEIGHBOUR'S FOWL, EATS IT AND THEN HAS THE AUDACITY TO COME TO COURT AND SWEAR INNOCENCE WITH A FEATHER OF THE FOWL STICKING IN HER HAIR.

THE MOMENT THE GUILTY WOMAN HEARD RAMA'S WORDS, SHE PASSED HER HAND OVER HER HAIR.

HOW COULD I HAVE BEEN SO CARELESS!

THE NEXT MOMENT —

SEIZE HER! SHE IS GUILTY.

THE SUSPECT STOOD SHAME-FACEDLY BEFORE RAMA.

YOU WILL REPLACE THE STOLEN BIRD AND PAY A HEAVY FINE TO THE COURT FOR UTTERING A FALSEHOOD UNDER OATH.

# THE DISHONEST DEBTOR

A FARMER ONCE SIGNED A BOND AND BORROWED A HUNDRED GOLD COINS FROM A MONEY-LENDER, PROMISING TO RETURN THE AMOUNT WITHIN THREE MONTHS.

AT THE END OF THE THREE MONTHS, THE MONEY-LENDER ASKED HIM TO REPAY THE SUM.

COME TO MY FARM TOMORROW WITH THE BOND AND I'LL RETURN THE AMOUNT ALONG WITH THE INTEREST.

THE MONEY-LENDER WENT THE NEXT DAY WITH THE BOND.

THERE SEEMS TO BE SOME MISTAKE ABOUT THE DATE. LET ME SEE THE BOND.

THE UNSUSPECTING MONEY-LENDER GAVE THE BOND TO HIM.

WHAT ARE YOU DOING?

I'M MAKING SURE THAT YOU'LL NEVER TROUBLE ME FOR THE MONEY AGAIN.

WHEN THE POOR MONEY-LENDER COMPLAINED TO MARYADA RAMA, HE SENT FOR THE FARMER.

WHY DID YOU TEAR UP THE BOND?

WHAT BOND, SIR? I KNOW NOTHING OF ANY BOND. THIS MAN IS A LIAR!

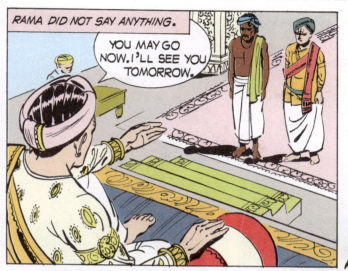

RAMA DID NOT SAY ANYTHING.

YOU MAY GO NOW. I'LL SEE YOU TOMORROW.

BUT THE MONEY-LENDER WILL NEVER SEE HIS GOLD.

LATER, RAMA SENT FOR THE MONEY-LENDER.

WHAT WAS THE SIZE OF THE BOND?

IT WAS ABOUT A SPAN LONG, SIR.

ALL RIGHT. NOW DO AS I SAY. WHEN I QUESTION YOU IN COURT TOMORROW INSIST THAT IT WAS A CUBIT*LONG.

AS YOU SAY, SIR.

THE NEXT DAY AT COURT—

THE PLAINTIFF IS UNDER OATH TO SPEAK NOTHING BUT THE TRUTH.

* 18"—22"

NOW TELL ME, WHAT WAS THE SIZE OF THE BOND YOU CLAIM WAS DESTROYED.

A CUBIT LONG, SIR.

THAT'S A BLATANT LIE! IT WAS ONLY A SPAN LONG.

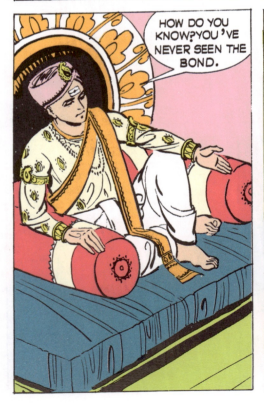

HOW DO YOU KNOW? YOU'VE NEVER SEEN THE BOND.

THE FARMER KNEW HE WAS TRAPPED AND CONFESSED.

YOU SHALL FIRST RETURN THE AMOUNT WITH INTEREST AND THEN GO TO PRISON.

# THE DEAD ELEPHANT AND THE BROKEN POTS

ONCE TWO MEN CAME TO MARYADA RAMA'S COURT.

WHAT IS THE MATTER?

SIR, THIS MAN BORROWED MY ELEPHANT FOR HIS SON'S WEDDING. THE ANIMAL DIED. I WANT MY ELEPHANT BACK ALIVE.

WHAT CAN I DO, SIR? THE ANIMAL SUDDENLY DIED. I OFFERED TO COMPENSATE HIM WITH MONEY BUT HE INSISTS THAT I RESTORE HIS ANIMAL TO LIFE AND RETURN IT.

RAMA TRIED TO PERSUADE THE PLAINTIFF TO ACCEPT THE MONEY BUT IN VAIN.

THE MAN IS A STUBBORN, UNREASONABLE FOOL. I'LL HAVE TO TEACH HIM A LESSON.

LET US POSTPONE THE CASE FOR A DAY. WE'LL TAKE UP THE MATTER AGAIN, TOMORROW.

AN HOUR LATER, HE SENT FOR THE DEFENDANT.

PILE UP ALL THE POTTERY YOU HAVE IN THE HOUSE, AGAINST YOUR DOOR TOMORROW. AND DON'T COME TO COURT TILL THE PLAINTIFF ARRIVES PERSONALLY TO CALL YOU.

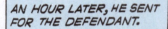
THE DEFENDANT IMMEDIATELY CAUGHT ON.

THE NEXT DAY, THE PLAINTIFF CAME TO COURT AT THE APPOINTED HOUR. BUT—

WE CANNOT TAKE UP YOUR CASE TILL THE DEFENDANT TOO IS HERE.

THAT SCOUNDREL! HE'S DELIBERATELY STAYED AWAY. I'LL GO AND BRING HIM.

HE RUSHED TO THE DEFENDANT'S HOUSE AND PUSHED THE DOOR.

TO HIS SURPRISE THERE WAS A LOUD CRASH.

WHAT HAVE YOU DONE?

MY PRECIOUS HEIRLOOMS, ALL DESTROYED! THEY HAVE BEEN IN OUR FAMILY FOR GENERATIONS.

PLEASE! PLEASE FORGIVE ME! I'LL PAY FOR THE DAMAGE.

I DON'T WANT MONEY. I WANT MY POTS BACK. I SHALL TAKE THE MATTER TO COURT.

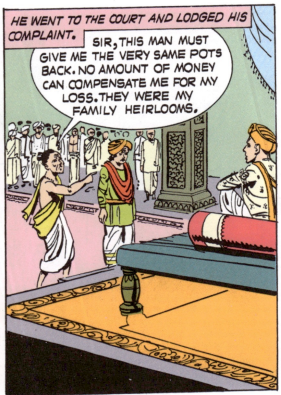

HE WENT TO THE COURT AND LODGED HIS COMPLAINT.

SIR, THIS MAN MUST GIVE ME THE VERY SAME POTS BACK. NO AMOUNT OF MONEY CAN COMPENSATE ME FOR MY LOSS. THEY WERE MY FAMILY HEIRLOOMS.

RAMA TURNED TO THE PLAINTIFF, NOW TURNED DEFENDANT.

HE WILL BRING YOUR ELEPHANT BACK TO LIFE THE DAY YOU RE-TURN, INTACT, THE VERY POTS YOU HAVE BROKEN. YOU MAY GO NOW.

# THE BRAHMAN'S GOLD

AN OLD BRAHMAN AND HIS WIFE ONCE DECIDED TO GO ON A PILGRIMAGE.

THEY PLACED ALL THEIR SAVINGS IN A BRASS POT AND FILLED IT WITH DAL.*

I'LL LEAVE IT WITH THE NEIGHBOURS FOR SAFE-KEEPING.

AT THE NEIGHBOUR'S HOUSE —

YOU MAY LEAVE IT IN THAT CORNER. NO ONE WILL TOUCH IT. TRUST ME.

ONE NIGHT, A FEW DAYS LATER, THE NEIGHBOURS HAD EIGHT UNEXPECTED GUESTS FOR DINNER.

WHAT SHALL I DO? I DON'T HAVE ANYTHING IN THE HOUSE. AND IT'S TOO LATE TO GO TO THE BAZAAR.

WE COULD BORROW SOME OF THE DAL FROM THE BRAHMAN'S POT AND REPLACE IT TOMORROW.

* SPLIT PULSES

AS HE POURED OUT THE DAL FROM THE POT —

WHAT'S THIS! GOLD COINS!

LET'S KEEP THE COINS AND FILL THE VESSEL WITH DAL.

GREED GOT THE BETTER OF THE MAN AND HE DID AS HIS WIFE SUGGESTED.

AS SOON AS THE BRAHMAN AND HIS WIFE RETURNED FROM THEIR PILGRIMAGE, THEY WENT NEXT DOOR FOR THE POT.

THERE YOU ARE! WE HAVEN'T EVEN MOVED IT FROM THAT CORNER.

THE BRAHMAN TOOK THE POT, WENT HOME, AND TIPPED OUT THE CONTENTS.

WHERE IS THE GOLD? THEY'VE STOLEN THE GOLD!

ALAS! WHAT WILL WE DO? WE ARE TOO OLD TO WORK.

THEY RAN BACK TO THE NEIGHBOUR.

PLEASE, PLEASE GIVE US OUR GOLD. WE'VE ALMOST STARVED OUR-SELVES TO SAVE IT. GIVE IT BACK TO US.

WHAT GOLD ARE YOU TALKING ABOUT? STOP MAKING A SCENE AT MY DOOR. WHAT WILL THE NEIGHBOURS THINK?

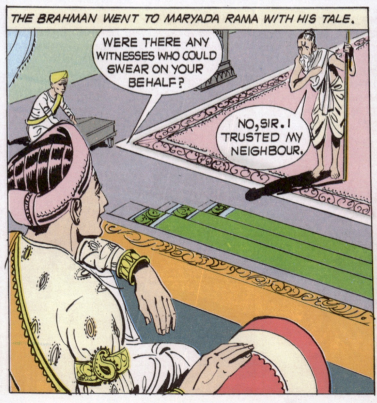

THE BRAHMAN WENT TO MARYADA RAMA WITH HIS TALE.

WERE THERE ANY WITNESSES WHO COULD SWEAR ON YOUR BEHALF?

NO, SIR. I TRUSTED MY NEIGHBOUR.

RAMA THOUGHT FOR A WHILE. THIS WAS A TRICKY CASE.

I HAVE IT!

GO HOME, MY GOOD MAN. YOU'LL SOON GET BACK YOUR GOLD.

HE SENT FOR A BASKET-MAKER.

I WANT A HOLLOW IDOL MADE OF CANE. IT SHOULD BE LARGE ENOUGH TO CONCEAL A CHILD AND LIGHT ENOUGH TO BE CARRIED BY TWO PEOPLE. COVER IT WITH LAC TO MAKE IT LOOK AS IF IT'S MADE OF WOOD.

WHEN THE IDOL WAS BROUGHT TO COURT, RAMA SENT FOR A BRIGHT CHILD.

NOW SIT HERE WITHOUT MAKING A SOUND AND LISTEN CAREFULLY TO WHATEVER YOU HEAR.

WHEN THE CHILD WAS COMFORTABLY SEATED INSIDE THE IDOL, RAMA SENT FOR THE NEIGHBOUR AND HIS WIFE.

CARRY THIS IDOL ROUND THE TEMPLE, SWEAR BEFORE GODDESS KÁLI THAT YOU HAVE NOT TAKEN THE BRAHMAN'S GOLD AND THEN COME BACK HERE.

TREMBLING WITH FEAR, THE COUPLE CARRIED THE IDOL TO THE TEMPLE AND BEGAN WALKING ROUND IT.

WHILE THEY WERE AT THE BACK OF THE TEMPLE AND OUT OF EARSHOT, AS HE BELIEVED, THE HUSBAND TURNED ANGRILY UPON HIS WIFE.

SEE WHAT YOU'VE DONE! WE'LL HAVE TO SWEAR TO A FALSEHOOD BEFORE THE GODDESS. SHE WILL NEVER FORGIVE US FOR IT.

INSIDE THE IDOL—

THE JUDGE WILL BE GLAD TO HEAR THIS.

AS SOON AS THE IDOL WAS BROUGHT BACK TO COURT, THE CHILD CAME OUT.

SIR, THIS MAN SAID TO HIS WIFE•••

AND THE CHILD REPEATED WHAT HE HAD HEARD.

KNOWING THAT HE WAS TRAPPED, THE NEIGHBOUR FELL ON HIS KNEES AND CONFESSED.

SEE THAT THEY RETURN THE GOLD AND SEND THEM TO PRISON.

# THE CAT'S PAW

ONCE A STRANGE CASE CAME UP BEFORE MARYADA RAMA.

THE PLAINTIFFS WERE THREE COTTON MERCHANTS AND THE DEFENDANT, THEIR FOURTH PARTNER.

SIR, THE FOUR OF US DEAL IN COTTON BALES. DISGUSTED WITH THE RAT MENACE WE BOUGHT A CAT.

"WE BECAME SO FOND OF THE CAT THAT EACH OF US TOOK CHARGE OF ONE OF ITS LEGS AND SHOWERED ATTENTION ON IT.

HERE IS A FINE ANKLET FOR MY LEG.

IT'S NOT AS FINE AS MINE.

"ONE DAY, THE CAT HURT ONE OF ITS LEGS—THE ONE BELONGING TO THE DEFENDANT.

MIAOW!

THERE! THERE! I'LL BIND IT WITH THIS OIL-SOAKED RAG AND IT WILL SOON BE ALL RIGHT.

"THAT NIGHT, AS THE CAT LIMPED ABOUT AFTER THE RATS, IT STEPPED ON AN OIL LAMP AND THE RAG CAUGHT FIRE.

"MAD WITH PAIN, IT DASHED HITHER AND THITHER AND SET ALL THE BALES ON FIRE.

"WHEN WE WOKE UP, IT WAS TOO LATE. ALL THE GOODS WERE DESTROYED.

SINCE IT WAS **HIS** LEG THAT CAUSED THE FIRE, HE WILL HAVE TO PAY FOR THE DAMAGES.

RAMA LOOKED AT THE DEFENDANT.

THE POOR FELLOW CANNOT BE BLAMED. IT WAS AN ACCIDENT. HIS PARTNERS MUST BE TAUGHT A LESSON.

HE TURNED TO THE PLAINTIFFS.

IT IS YOU IN FACT WHO WILL HAVE TO MAKE GOOD TO THE DEFENDANT THE VALUE OF ONE FOURTH OF THE GOODS DESTROYED. FOR···

···IT WAS THE SOUND LEGS THAT HELPED THE CAT JUMP ABOUT AND SET FIRE TO THE BALES.

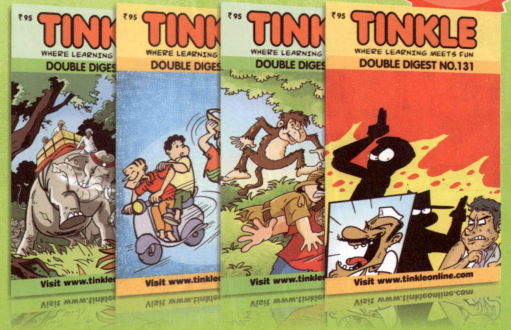